For Janetta and Jude – with love and thanks
for your support over many years

Text and illustrations copyright © Jude Daly 2017

The right of Jude Daly to be identified as the author and illustrator
of this work has been asserted by her in accordance with the Copyright,
Designs and Patents Act, 1988 (United Kingdom).

First published in Great Britain and in the USA in 2017 by
Otter-Barry Books
Little Orchard, Burley Gate, Hereford, HR1 3QS

www.otterbarrybooks.com

A catalogue record for this book is available from the British Library.

ISBN 978-1-91095-942-8

Illustrated with acrylic
Printed in China

1 3 5 7 9 8 6 4 2

# SIX BLIND MICE AND AN ELEPHANT

## JUDE DALY

Otter-Barry BOOKS

One hot, hot day,
a sleepy elephant wandered
out of the forest and into
a farmer's barn.

He sniffed around,
made himself a cosy bed,
sighed contentedly
and fell asleep.

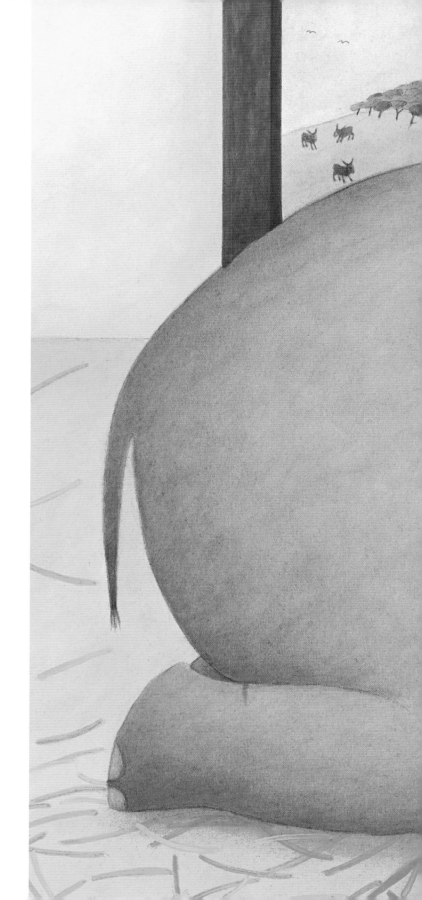

The farmer had always wanted to see a real elephant.
He beckoned excitedly to his wife and children
and they all ran out to look. Then they called the
neighbours. Soon the barn was surrounded by men,
women and children, all whispering to each other
about **the wonder of an elephant**.

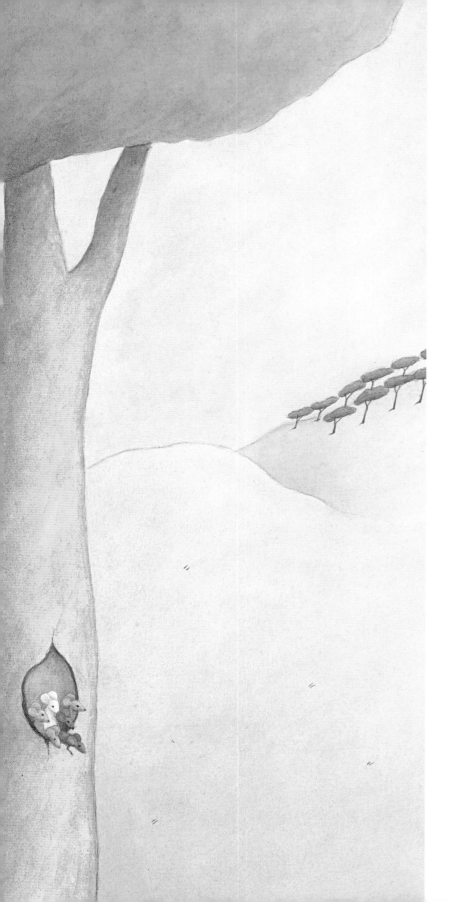

Six blind mice, dozing in their nest, were woken by a most unusual smell, a scent they had never smelled before.

**What could it be?**

They just had to find out.

As they crept along, following their noses, they smelled lots of things they knew about:

    chickens,

       cows,

          pigs,

             people,

                dogs

                   and. . .

# CATS!

"Help!" squealed the mice, and scurried into a hidey-hole.

While they were hiding, the six blind mice overheard people talking about a remarkable creature called an **elephant**, that was sleeping in the farmer's barn.

And the more the mice heard, the more they knew this **must** be the creature they were looking for.

So, as soon as all the people and all the animals – especially the cat – went away, the mice cｒｅｐt out of their hole and set off again.

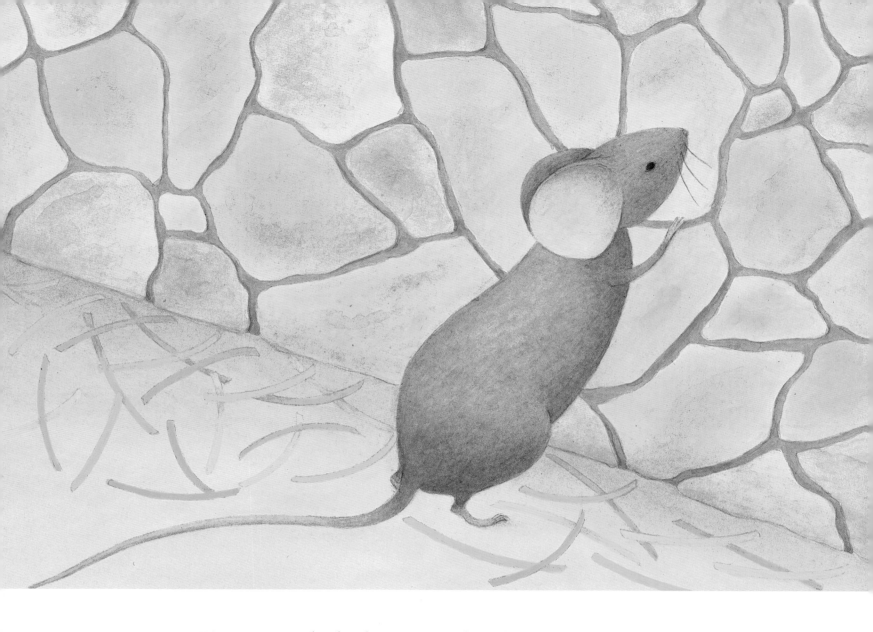

First to reach the barn was the oldest blind mouse.
He scampered inside and almost crashed into
the elephant's gigantic, **solid side.**

*"Ouch!"* he squealed. "Why did no one say that
an elephant is like a – **wall?**"

"Because it is **not**," squeaked the second mouse, as she scuttled up and down the elephant's smooth, sharp tusk. "An elephant is actually like a – **spear!**"

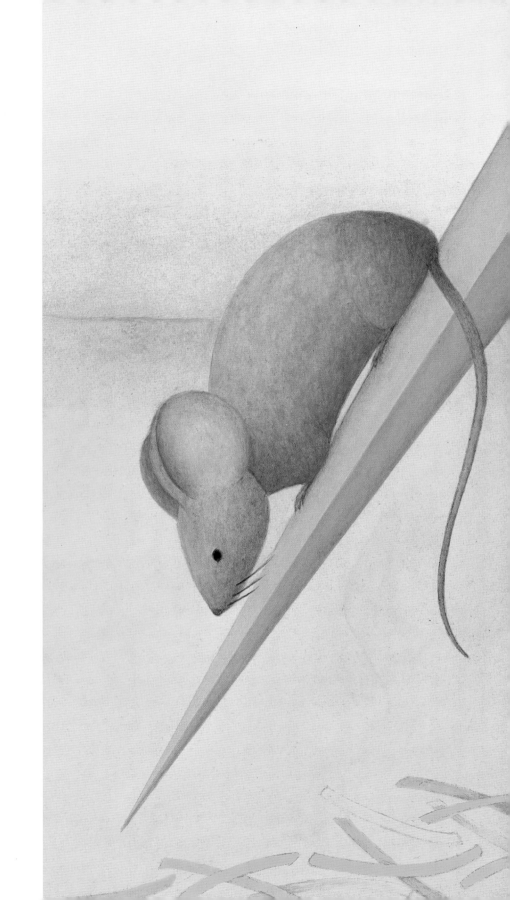

The third mouse, who was busy exploring the elephant's ear, piped up.

"That's really silly! It is all too clear to see that an elephant is like a – **fan!**"

Suddenly, the elephant stood up and scratched his ear with such gusto that some of the mice let go of him while others held on for dear life.

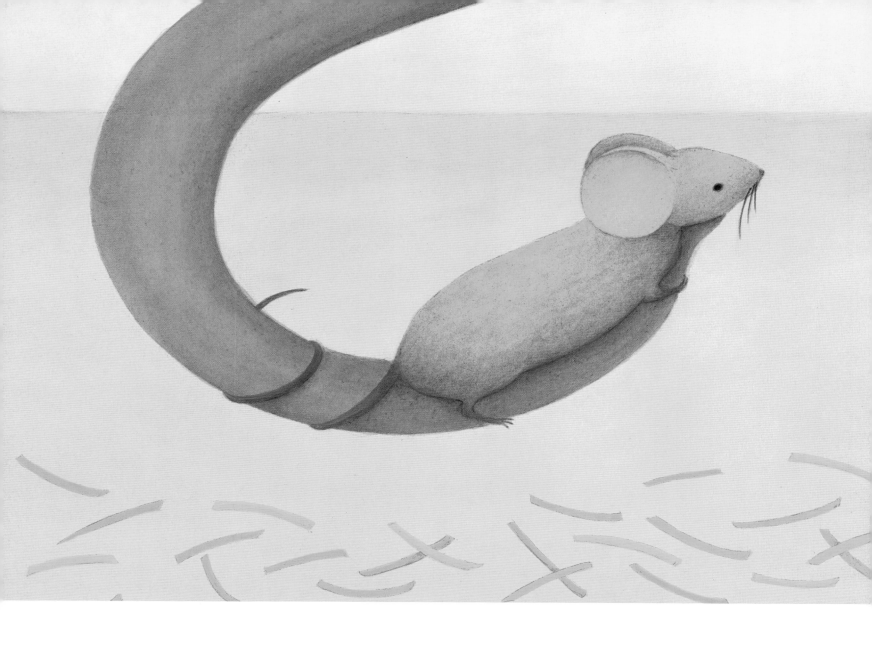

The fourth blind mouse managed to cling on to the elephant's trunk as it twisted this way and that. "A fan, what nonsense!" he squealed. "This creature is very like a – **snake!**"

"A snake?" squeaked the fifth mouse, as he scuttled around a knotty knee. "How ridiculous! Why, even the blindest mouse could tell you that an elephant is like a – **tree!**"

"Hey, everyone!" called the sixth
and youngest blind mouse,
hanging from the elephant's tail.
"You are all wrong!  I'll tell you
exactly what an elephant is like."

The other mice crept closer.
Why, even the elephant himself
seemed to be listening!

"An elephant is like . . .

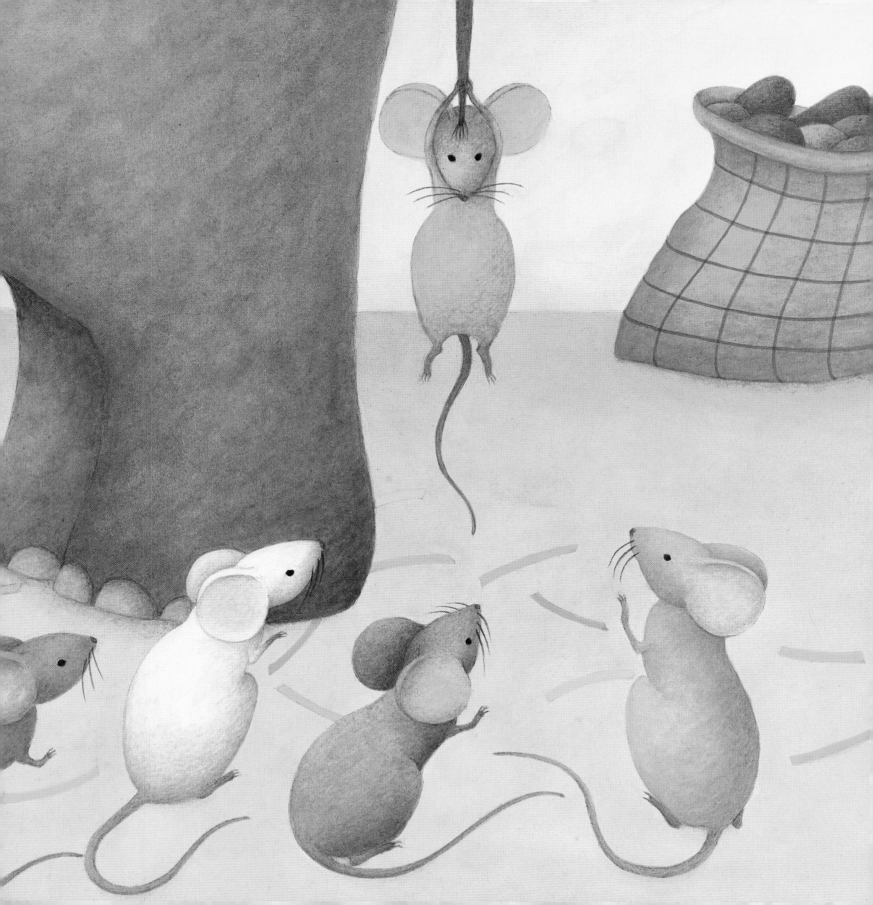

an elephant is exactly like a – **rope!**"

There was a moment's silence.

Then the sleepy elephant
flapped his ears and
trumpeted so loudly that
all six mice scurried for cover.

"Oh dear!" said the elephant softly. "I really did not mean to scare you. Please come back. I just wanted to say that each of you is a little bit right.

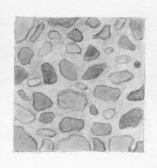 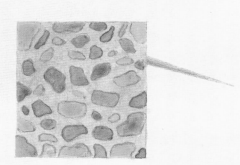 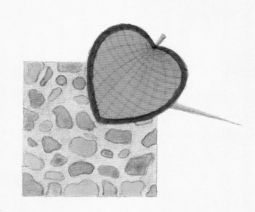

I am **large** and **solid** with sharp tusks and big fan-like ears.

And I have to agree that my legs are like tree-trunks,
my nose is long and bendy and my tail could be mistaken
for a rope. But, when all is said and done, my friends,
I am exactly like...

**an elephant!**"

Then the elephant yawned.

"A very beautiful elephant," the oldest blind mouse squeaked quietly.

"A very tired elephant!" the youngest mouse chipped in.

And the elephant rumbled with laughter until he
fell
    fast
       asleep.

So the six blind mice tiptoed out of the barn.

Then they scampered back to their nest, squeaking and squealing with satisfaction at having seen for themselves **the wonder of an elephant**.

## ABOUT THE STORY

This fable originated in India. It has crossed between many
religious traditions and is part of Jain, Buddhist, Sufi and Hindu lore.
In the 19th Century the American poet John Godfrey Saxe's
splendid poem, *The Blind Men and the Elephant*,
helped to popularise the story. In several versions,
including John Godfrey Saxe's, no agreement is reached.
But I did not like to leave my blind mice
never knowing the full wonder of an elephant!

*Jude Daly*